Penguin

and the

cupcake

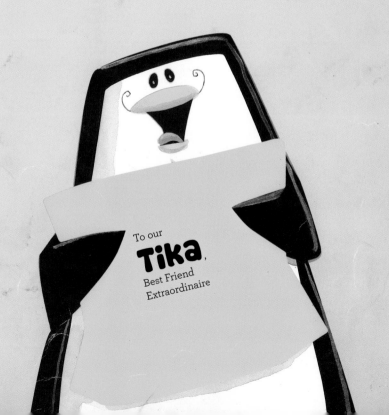

To our
Tika,
Best Friend
Extraordinaire

First published in 2008 by Simply Read Books
www.simplyreadbooks.com

Text & Illustrations © 2008 Ashley Spires

Library and Archives Canada Cataloguing in Publication

Spires, Ashley, 1978-
            Penguin and the cupcake / written and illustrated by Ashley Spires.
Interest age level: Ages 3 to 7.
ISBN 978-1-897476-04-8
            I. Title.
PS8637.P57P46 2008   jC813'.6   C2008-901245-3

We gratefully acknowledge the suppport of the Canada Council of the Arts, the
Government of Canada through the Book Publishing Industry Development Program
and the BC Arts Council for our publishing program.

Book design by Robin Mitchell-Cranfield for hundreds & thousands

Printed in Singapore

10 9 8 7 6 5 4 3 2 1

PENGUIN

and the

cupcake

totally made up by
ASHLEY SPIRES

Simply Read Books

Hi! I'm Penguin.

I know what you're thinking: what's a penguin doing in a book with a walrus and a polar bear?

Everyone knows that penguins live waaaaay down south in Antarctica and walruses and polar bears live waaaaay up north in the Arctic.

So how did we end up in a book together? Let me tell you...

It all started one day when my buddies and I were hanging out at the fish hole. Now, I'm not one to complain, but for the last one thousand, four hundred and seventy-three days I've eaten fish.

 Sure, I get to toss in some krill,

 maybe a squid now and again for flavor,

 but there are some foods you can't find in the sea. Say, for instance —

 CUPCAKES!!

Note: Many species of fish are endangered because humans are over-fishing the oceans. Penguins are having a hard time finding food, which is another reason that Penguin was eager to find something else to eat. Though looking for a cupcake was probably not the healthiest choice.

My pal told me that his sister's friend's cousin is living the good life eating cupcakes in this place called the Northern Hemisphere.

So I decided to head north to find some cupcakes. When I was all packed up and ready to go, I spread my wings and took to the sky.

But penguins can't fly!

You can tell the story but only if you tell it correctly. Now tell the truth or we will have to take over.

Fine.

It's not our turn?

As I was saying, I took to the sky.

It was a **long** and **difficult** journey. A lesser penguin would not have made it.

But I knew I would soon arrive to a new land of **possibilities, opportunities,**

lots and lots of **cupcakes** and...

SNOW!?!

It couldn't be! I had traveled so far just to visit more snow! Nevertheless I was still determined to find the fabled cupcakes. I set out in search of my sugary goal.

Soon, I came upon a very purple local.

Hello! I'm Penguin.

Do you
know
where
I can find
some

cupcakes?

Oh no. I don't eat cupcakes. All that sugar goes straight to my third chin. I'm on a strict kelp diet.

Note: Walruses don't eat kelp. They mostly eat bivalve mollusks (a fancy word for clams and mussels). Unfortunately, this walrus has self-esteem issues. She was trying to meet an unrealistic physical ideal. All she really needed to do was love herself.

I said **goodbye** to Walrus and set off once again. It wasn't long before I ran into another local.

Hi there!

Note:
This is
one of the
few large
patches of
ice left
where
Polar Bear
can chill.

The Arctic
ice cap is
melting
because,
among
other things,
Penguin
and too
many people
fly in
air-polluting
planes.

Hello. I'm Penguin.

Hello. I'm Polar Bear.

I'm searching for **cupcakes.** Can you help me?

Sorry, I don't eat cupcakes. I'm more into blubbery things like seals and beluga whales. Sometimes I even eat birds. Hey, aren't you a bird?

I'm usually a pretty calm guy—Danger's my middle name—so don't get the wrong idea about me when you see what happened next...

eeeeeeeeeeee e e e e e e e e e e e e e e e e e e e e e e!

I was beat. The stories of cupcakes were clearly exaggerated. With a heavy heart, I decided to take a plane home.

Because **penguins** can't fly.

They know that already! And just because I can't fly doesn't mean I can't swim the pants off both of you!

We don't wear pants.

Please go away.

But all was not lost. Suddenly there was a heavenly voice beside me...

Behold, an angel in pearls handed me a pink icing-topped

cupcake!

I opened my beak and gobbled the whole cupcake down. I hardly got icing on my feathers.

It was pure **bliss!**

The kind lady could tell I was itching for more.

Would you like the **whole box**, dear?

Thank you!

I returned triumphantly to my home and my friends. While we shared the cupcakes I told them of Walrus, Polar Bear and the kind lady. We were almost finished when something fell out of the box...

That's it? We only had a few lines!

Fine with me. I'm sick of this book.

After all this talk of food, I need a snack.

I hope they remember to pay me in kelp.